LONDON

Edited By Kat Cockrill

First published in Great Britain in 2019 by:

 Young**Writers**

Young Writers
Remus House
Coltsfoot Drive
Peterborough
PE2 9BF
Telephone: 01733 890066
Website: www.youngwriters.co.uk

FOREWORD

Welcome, Reader!

Are you ready to step back in time? Then come right this way - your time-travelling machine awaits! It's very simple, all you have to do is turn the page and you'll be transported to the past! WOW!

Is it magic? Is it a trick? No! It's all down to the skill and imagination of primary school pupils from around the country. We gave them the task of writing a story about any time in history, and to do it in just 100 words! I think you'll agree they've achieved that brilliantly – this book is jam-packed with exciting and thrilling tales from the past.

These young authors have brought history to life with their stories. This is the power of creativity and it gives us life too! Here at Young Writers we want to pass our love of the written word onto the next generation and what better way to do that than to celebrate their writing by publishing it in a book!

It sets their work free from homework books and notepads and puts it where it deserves to be – out in the world and preserved forever! Each awesome author in this book should be super proud of themselves, and now they've got proof of their imagination, their ideas and their creativity in black and white, to look back on in years to come when their first experience of publication is an ancient adventure itself!

Now I'm off to dive through the timelines and pick some winners – it's going to be difficult to choose, but I'm going to have a lot of fun along the way. I may even learn some new history facts too!

Kat

CONTENTS

Caspian-James Leonard Phillips (10) 37

Real Action Butterfly School, Queens Park

Ayman Mohamed (11)	38
Nathan Melaka (7)	39
Amir Azimi (10)	40
Rebeca Mare (9)	41
Yeabsira Tegenu (7)	42
Anamika Shaw (9)	43
Alex Read (10)	44
Naomi Kassa (9)	45

Roe Green Junior School, Brent

Malaika Raja (9)	46
Abdullah Ibnu Muhammad (9)	47
Shadar Wilson (9)	48

St James' CE Junior School, Forest Gate

Tayyab Ahmed Hussain (10)	49
Aleena Ahmed (10)	50
Tahreema Jwardar (9)	51
Jihan Waasil (9)	52
Aritz Ayomikun Akinrele (8)	53
Eliza Emini (11)	54
Fabia Isabele Svetlikauskaite (10)	55
Arianna Ahmed (11)	56
Ihsaan Mujaddid Uzzaman (8)	57
Rose Boadi (11)	58
Bubacari Dembaga (10)	59
Ismail Muhammad (10)	60
Hajar Bennebri (10)	61
Amirah Mahreen Begum (8)	62
Caleb Barnieh (10)	63
Aniyah Wilson Opoku (9)	64

Ashmal Khan (10)	65
Soloman Rehan (10)	66
Ivet Penovska (8)	67
Saifan Khan (9)	68
Andrea Boateng (10)	69
Russell Casey Addotey (9)	70
Liyana Haque (8)	71
Matyas Sarosi (10)	72
Ramaiya Princess Payne Fearon (8)	73
Edward Osie Kwame (8)	74
Aleena Hoque (8)	75
Hima Subair (9)	76
Anayet Noor (10)	77
Kayla Monica Monteiro (10)	78
Nisha Kaur (10)	79
Maria Camila Galarza (10)	80
Aysha Begum (11)	81
Perla Alegra Petkeviciute (7)	82
Jojo Sam (8)	83
Tyrese Henry (8)	84
Daniel Mazose (8)	85
Alisa Emini (8)	86
Mantas Kairys (9)	87
Manuela Tami Adamu Adegbenro (10)	88
Aisha Saddiq (10)	89
Rahell Noori (10)	90
Farhan Omar Kazi (8)	91
Yahyah Islam (10)	92

St John's Highbury Vale, Highbury

Adam Bogdanowicz Bower (8)	93

St Mark's CE Primary School, Lambeth

Ryan Laurent Xavier   94
Ssimbwa (10)

St Nicholas School, Brent

Thomas Bignone (9)   95
Mayon Wanniarachchige (10)   96
Jumana Mahmud (10)   97

St Paul's CE Primary School, Winchmore Hill

George Christodoulou (8)   98
Isaac Dempsey (9)   99

The Japanese School in London, Acton

Osuke Ueda (10)   100
Julie Marumoto (9)   101
Joseph Duxbury (9)   102
Chika Tsunoda (10)   103
Aiko Groves (9)   104
Minori Muramatsu (9)   105
Mai Akakura (10)   106
Kyo Adachi Mavromichalis (9)   107

THE
MINI SAGAS

'HE CAME, HE SAW, HE CONKED US'!

Temple Terror

Emma was on her way home when she found a big floating hole. Emma looked at the hole, confused. *What a weird hole?* she thought. Then she looked down the road to make sure no one was around and quickly jumped into the mysterious hole. Soon, she found herself in ancient Rome. In front of Emma was the Abandoned Temple. People said there were mummies and zombies inside. Emma went into the dark room and saw some gold. Emma took the gold but a zombie and mummy came. So Emma ran but she was never to be seen again!

Jemima Oluwaseyitan Ojelade (7)
Boxgrove Primary School, Abbeywood

The Black Hole

One night, office worker, Jetmir, was working late. He had a night shift and was printing something for his boss. The printer did not work. He checked the ink and there was no ink left. He decided to get some ink from the storage room to refill the ink tank. Right when he was about to step in, there was a black hole! Then he realised it was the ink. He took a step inside and he was in Roman times! He looked around, he was in the Colosseum! He couldn't believe it, it was a surprise!

Briana Lacaj (8)
Boxgrove Primary School, Abbeywood

The Sandy Adventure

Once upon a time, there was a boy called James. Suddenly, he fell into a deep, mysterious hole. James saw a glowing portal and walked through. It was filled with luxurious temples and statues! James snuck into the temple. As he went to touch a piece of gold, doors slammed, windows crashed. A mummy apocalypse! They tied him to the wall. Then the mummies used their powers and turned James into stone. James should have learnt his lesson by now not to walk into strange places...

Lily Cheeseman (8)
Boxgrove Primary School, Abbeywood

Rise Of The Women

One boiling, midsummer morning, Tutankhamun was reporting to his kingly business when a mosquito bit him and he dropped dead.

The next day, Cleopatra was due to take the throne but when she woke up, she was in prison! "Help!" Cleopatra cried.

Days turned into weeks, weeks turned into months and months turned into years. "I'm supposed to be ruling Egypt!" she shouted to herself. Suddenly, Cleopatra discovered a key. It was her ticket out of there! Cleopatra could rightfully take the throne! The women could rise! Whoever was ruling now would go to prison forever and ever and ever!

Daisy-Mae Sherry (9)
Brunswick Park Primary School, Camberwell

There's A Time Machine In My Clubhouse!

One summer's day, Hana woke up hearing her mother screaming, "Get dressed, Hana, your friends are here!" So Hana rushed downstairs to see Bella and Rian.
"We're going to the clubhouse now!" Bella whispered, "I found a time machine!" Hana, Bella and Rian rushed to the clubhouse and gazed at the time machine. They all jumped into the time machine and went back to the dinosaurs. The first T-rex was huge, Hana and her friends smiled. Hana's dream finally came true!
They cheered, "Yay!"

Akpevwe Ogueh (9)
Brunswick Park Primary School, Camberwell

Beware Of The Dinosaur

It was a dark, gloomy day with no bright yellow sun in the sky. There was a boy called Jack who lived with his mum. As Jack woke up, he heard a terrible noise that sounded like a stomp from a gigantic, alive, green dinosaur. "I'm out of here!" he screamed. All of a sudden, Jack saw the vast green dinosaur trying to bite his legs off! Unexpectedly, the dirty black mud was shaking and it covered the large green dinosaur. All of a sudden, Jack saw the wonderful Tutankhamun but then he drank from his cup and passed out.

Zack Quijano-Reed (9)
Brunswick Park Primary School, Camberwell

Tomb Of Doom

"Help!" I shouted as I got pushed into King Tut's tomb. "Worst trip ever!" I waited until the laughter stopped. I opened the tomb to discover I was in the Valley of the Kings. The room was filled with murals. I ran out of the pyramid into the jungle. Where was my class? The ground shook. It was a dinosaur! Maybe he wouldn't see me. *Ring! Ring!* He heard it and ran towards me. I needed somewhere to hide. I came to a cliff, I had no choice but to jump. Was I ever going to find my class?

Cordell Henriques-Alfred (9)

Brunswick Park Primary School, Camberwell

Death Stare

Once upon a time, there was an old man, he was very ill and didn't have enough mouldy, disgusting bread to cure him. He lived in ancient Egypt, next to the River Nile. The old man was a farmer who worked very hard. As quick as a flash, it turned to night. He went to bed extremely exhausted and weak. In the gloomy night, a dark soul took over him and turned him evil to kill people. He rose from his bed like a ghost, his eyes were cold and ghastly. His Death Stare was waiting for their first victim.

Sienna Rae Tipple (9)
Brunswick Park Primary School, Camberwell

Time Trouble

Eliza woke up to the sound of firecrackers. It was, in fact, her father inventing a teleporter in the garden shed. She slid down the banister and unlocked the door. She climbed onto the little seat and set off. She ended up in the time when the Celts were at war with the Romans. Boudicca, the leader of the Iceni tribe was informing her soldiers of her new plan. Suddenly, *boom! Crash! Pow!* The Romans started to attack from every angle. Eliza ran back to the teleporter and travelled back home. She then fell back fast asleep on her bed.

Suhayla Islam (8)
Buttercup Primary School, Whitechapel

When Man Used Rocks

The wind hit my face as I plummeted towards Earth, ejected from a time machine. I landed on the ground with a thud and narrowly missed being injured by a rock. I turned around and saw an angry caveman hurtling stones towards me. I ran for my life, searching for the time machine as I went. Finally, I spotted it and threw myself into the time machine. Moments later, I was back in my messy bedroom. "Guys! I'm back!" I called as I went downstairs, finding my family in the position I'd left them in. No time had passed.

Maariya Islam (11)
Buttercup Primary School, Whitechapel

'You're Captured!'

Roars filled the land with fear. Flames glimmered and blood carpeted the floor. I was being chased by a band of berserkers! I took cover behind a rough wall of bricks alongside me. I finally lost sight of the berserkers. I had lost sight of my parents in the chase. I then found them behind a bush. Me, the captor, my father and mother snuck through the woods and we jumped over the hedge. The captor drew out his sword. He then held us at knifepoint, so we surrendered. "You're captured!" he said. He was a Viking!

Yaseen Hussain (10)
Buttercup Primary School, Whitechapel

The King Who Chopped Off Heads

Long ago, a king lived in a humungous castle. The king chopped off heads if they did anything wrong to him. There also lived a man who wanted some money so, at night, he went to the king's castle and stole money.

The next day, the king realised money had gone from his bank. The king told his servant to go and search for the person who took some money. The servant found the man and the servant chopped off the man's head viciously and angrily. The king and the servant lived happily ever since that day!

Asiya Abdalle (9)
Buttercup Primary School, Whitechapel

Hair Today, Abyssinia Tomorrow

150 years ago, my great-great-grandfather, Emperor Tewodros of Abyssinia, was taken hostage by the English. He died in captivity. The English troops snipped two locks of hair from his head and triumphantly took them back to England. They were sealed away at the British Army Museum. As I walked towards that very place, it was as if Tewodros himself was whispering to me. "Avenge me, Hirut, bring our country triumph and preserve your family's reputation!" A sudden feeling of courage flooded through me. I marched through the doors, ready to confront the curator and make my family proud!

Lucy Whitehead (9)
Dulwich Wood Primary School, Dulwich

Who Would Win?

As the full moon came, the four dragon athletes came to race. They waited and waited for the baa of the sheep, it signalled the start of the race. The begging came. The dragons blew fire, angrily. Crane and Jrio swooped first, taking the lead. Ilias and Rino took the lead with Ilias screaming impatiently. Helos and Croit blew fire to Jrio's and his rider fell to the ground. Everyone pushed and shoved each other. It was the last lap. They tried harder and harder to get people out. The dragons were losing strength. Who would fall down?

Abdulmatin Emilola (10)
Dulwich Wood Primary School, Dulwich

Crazy Cleopatra

One day, a young-looking woman named Cleopatra was taking a walk by an extremely stinky rubbish bin that was surrounded by flies. When Cleopatra's walk was coming to an end, five children began to hold their noses and laugh. Her feet began stomping on the floor. She was enraged. When her stroll came to an end, Cleopatra got in the bath four times to remove the smell but it stuck to her like glue. The stench grew worse, as did the bullying, until one day she got so fed up that she called Genie who banished the mean kids forever.

Lacey Mahoney (10)
Dulwich Wood Primary School, Dulwich

Watch Out For The Rats!

The streets of London, my happy place. The place you can be free. You can listen to the bustling of the streets like the birds tweeting their sweet song. I skipped along without a care in the world. I rushed off, excited at the sight of a scarlet blouse. I darted around the people who gossiped their heads off. As I stepped into the shop, I could smell the brand-new clothes wafting in the air. Alarmingly, a shopkeeper shrieked and fell facedown. I heard screams and several people on the floor. There was a rat!

Akachi Daniella Oti (9)
Dulwich Wood Primary School, Dulwich

The Secret Of The Brontë Sisters

The wind blew my hair into my face. My diary was tightly clenched in my fist, a fresh draft of 'Agnes Grey' safe on my person. Me and Charlotte would prove what women could do once and for all. My publisher's office smelt funny. All warm, like coffee, yet cold like ice. I could see his top hat from over his newspaper. He looked up and saw us in front of him. He froze in shock but I could see his usual frown turn upside down. We had proven girls could be writers. Hopefully, it will stay that way...

Mia Brol (10)
Dulwich Wood Primary School, Dulwich

Dinosaur Beast

As daylight was coming to an end, I looked through my window. Suddenly, I ran screaming like I had never screamed before. I went outside. *Roar!* I clenched my hands so tight, I was gasping for breath. I ran for my life as they were still behind me, ready to eat. I never gave up. I did not know what it was but, the quicker I ran, the more this beast came for me. It wouldn't give up. I ran quicker and then I knew, it was a dinosaur!

Lucas Mesfin (9)
Dulwich Wood Primary School, Dulwich

The Knights Of The Blue Forest

Many years ago, there were two knights called Sir Michael the Brave and Sir Trian the Strong. One rainy night, coming back from a fair, they stopped at an inn. There, they overhead two assassins, Scarface and Clawhook, say that they wanted to kill King Louis.

That night, Sir Michael and Sir Trian were on the lookout for invaders. Suddenly, Scarface and Clawhook snuck up and attacked them. Sir Michael was fast and stabbed Clawhook in the heart while Sir Trian threw Scarface off the tower.

The next day, King Louis rewarded both of them with medals of bravery!

Michael Wilson (9)
Laidlaw Education, Chiswick

Over The Top

"You're going over!" the captain's voice startled me as I lay, chewing corned beef, possibly the least nutritious food ever. Taunted by images of tortured soldiers, I was paralysed with fear until the shrill screech of the whistle shattered the silence, jolting me back to reality. Terror bottled up inside as I went over. Scrambling through the mud of no-man's-land, I felt a gunshot whizz past me and a shell explode beside me. I was smothered in sloppy mud by the time I reached enemy lines. A bolt of pain shot through me. I collapsed. Would I make it home?

Keya Shah (11)
Norfolk House School, Muswell Hill

Troy

Smoke. Heat. Screams. The sound of swords clashing brought me to my senses and I ran from the flames that were quickly enveloping my house, half-blinded by smoke. The Achaean soldiers fought like Titans, their armour flashing as they stormed through Troy, leaving a trail of dead Trojans behind them. I couldn't see my family anywhere. I was alone. All of a sudden, an Achaean warrior jumped in front of me, his sword raised menacingly. He glared at me, heartlessly, his armour glinting in the firelight. I turned and ran faster than I ever had before, never looking back...

Holly Piccinin (11)
Norfolk House School, Muswell Hill

The Raid Of Tutankhamun's Tomb

Tom invaded the tomb and the door shut, eerily. He was plunged into darkness. The light from his candle cast shadows that danced along the walls. Miraculously, he detected gold and scooped up a handful. Instantly, the sarcophagus slid open and Tutankhamun's mummy bolted upright! Tom's smile dropped from his face like a theatrical mask, replaced by a look of sheer terror! Tom frantically spied for an exit and flew for it. A corridor of spears emerged. He found himself dodging spears from all angles. Wearily, he stepped out of the tomb to be blinded by sunlight...

Leo Irvine (11)
Norfolk House School, Muswell Hill

The Slaughter Of East France

Miserable, horrible, disgusting. I've heard those words many times before. Me and my fellow group of soldiers sat in the trenches, guns loaded and ready. We saw a lone red flare light up the dull grey sky like a small red sun ascending all the time. Then the gunfire came like a round of staccato notes, while screams accompanied it a few seconds later. The firing went on for a couple of minutes until it suddenly stopped. This was our chance. We leapt up out of the trenches, already sprinting forward. We advanced through the battlefield, advanced to freedom...

Sidney Embleton (10)
Norfolk House School, Muswell Hill

On My Own

Ugrott was feeling upset because he couldn't hunt by himself. One day, he was watching his brother, Zorge, hunt a deer when he heard a rumbling noise. Turning around, Ugrott saw a huge buffalo. "Zorge!" he cried. Zorge turned around to shout at Ugrott and saw the buffalo. Dropping his bow and arrow, he ran for his life. Ugrott then had one of his amazing, caveman ideas. He picked up the weapons and climbed a tree. He aimed. He shot the arrow right into the buffalo's neck. The buffalo was dead. He had saved Zorge! He was finally a hero!

Amelie Blair (11)
Norfolk House School, Muswell Hill

Guy Fawkes' Last Hour

The ropes cut into my wrists, my hands were numb. Omnipotent dread engulfed me as I stepped upon the gallows. We wanted freedom. Instead, we were in chains. Plotting, hiding, subterfuge. Dingy nights heaving barrels of gunpowder into Parliament's cellars to rid us of the traitorous monarch, James. Torch in hand, ready to ignite, I heard Catesby's footsteps but, alas! It was betrayal in royal uniform! "Killer! Assassin!" Insults and torture, I bid you farewell as I hail Death with his horse. Burn me on the bonfire, for God is my fuel!

Christopher Sergeant (10)
Norfolk House School, Muswell Hill

A Day In The Life Of A Chimney Sweep

In I go! I thought to myself, *Why am I so nervous to climb? I sweep chimneys all the time!* I brushed my thoughts away and tried to focus on the job at hand. I got up. As soon as I was a few metres in, my lungs started closing up. I coughed, spluttering in the dark. My head pounded and my heart thumped inside my weary chest. I looked up into the endless soot. I prepared to say my goodbyes, just as a hand grabbed me, saving me. I called out, "Timmy!"

Eva Brown (10)
Norfolk House School, Muswell Hill

The Apollo I Disaster

Once, one or two decades ago, NASA had made an amazing, mind-blowing decision. They would send a rocket to the moon! I know what you're thinking, they lost their minds. That is not the best bit yet. Oh no, it was not the best bit. There would be three men who would walk on the moon! They went through extremely intense training. They trained all day long. Finally, the day came, it was the day of destiny, take-off day!

"Five... four... three... two... one..."

Kaboom! The rocket exploded. There was a gasp and, obviously, a funeral.

Jim Mulholland (8)
North Ealing Primary School, Ealing

History Hurricane

A tourist was walking down the street when a hurricane came. He ran and he could feel the power and speed of the natural disaster. Suddenly, the man was swept off his feet into the eye of the storm. As he was spinning, he saw the weirdest sight. There was a real-life pharaoh in front of him! And a Saxon, Celt, Boudicca, a neanderthal, the first Homo sapien, knights and other historical people! Just then, the storm died and the man was flung to the ground. He never spoke of it again, thinking that people would not believe him.

Harriet Wood (8)
North Ealing Primary School, Ealing

The Romans Are Here!

Stomp! Stomp! Stomp! The police were alerting us to stay alert! When I was looking through the window, there was a big group of men marching through Pitshanger Lane. People were getting killed. I knew they were Roman soldiers because they wore sandals made of iron and they wore red shirts under their armour and they were shouting, "Dex sin! Dex sin!" Suddenly, the Romans came to my house and they took all the children and they took us back in time. Suddenly, we got sold and Emperor Caesar bought us...

Kimika Fukui (8)
North Ealing Primary School, Ealing

The Dinosaur

The wind howled and then I heard the distant roar. I hid in a nearby cave for shelter but I knew it wouldn't be long before the terrifying beast found me. My heart thumped as I heard footsteps drawing nearer. Louder and louder they became until I came face-to-face with a dinosaur. His jaw was the size of my head and he probably could have swallowed me whole. I stood there, frozen to the ground, heart struck. His beady eyes looked at me as though he was scanning to see if I was edible. I gulped, petrified...

Esme Walker (10)
North Ealing Primary School, Ealing

The Trenches

The wind howled, the rain dropped and I ran like never before. The gunshots and the squishing of my shoes were loud as I was in the trenches. My heart beat angrily as I ran to shoot the enemy. I finally stopped because I reached the damp, wet place I needed to be. I quickly loaded my bullets and prepared my gun. The crack of my gun as I knelt down. I took my last shot, I could hear the ringing of my gun. It soared through the barren, lifeless, mouldy, red landscape. I was in World War One.

Livia Cox (10)
North Ealing Primary School, Ealing

Egyptian Nightmare

No, this couldn't be! I had woken up to find myself
in the desert. A minute ago, I was reading a
paragraph about how ancient Egyptians lived and,
ta-da, I got magicked here. I could see the
pyramids! "Wow, you scared me!" I said. Egyptians
had appeared.

"We made everything better than Stonehenge,
better than anything!" said the Egyptians. I couldn't
believe it was an ancient Egyptian talking to me.
"So, how do I get back?" I asked.

"You can't go into the future..." Did he just say I
can't go back to the future?

Jamila Chowdhery (9)
Olga Primary School, Tower Hamlets

The Truth Of The Great Fire Of London

In Pudding Lane, in a unique bakery, a small flame started. It slowly got bigger and bigger. The fire alarm went off, suddenly, explosions started. Everyone in the bakery got trapped, they couldn't find the source of the fire. They had no choice. They had to expect death. *Boom!* The bakery had exploded, everyone had to evacuate. They called the firefighters to come and put the fire out. Everyone was shocked after that tragic event. They had to build new homes, towns and farms. They wished it never happened. Now, people say it was planned.

Joshua Lucas Harron-Jones (10)
Olga Primary School, Tower Hamlets

Felix's Story

I am Felix, a Roman soldier. This is my story about the attempt to invade Britain. When I found out that I was going, I was terrified. Some soldiers were happy, I don't know why. We could be killed! We went by sea. I felt sick, I wasn't sure if it was nerves or seasickness. I felt more nervous than I ever had before. When we finally arrived, the battle started straight away because the Celts were waiting for us. We were tired and sick from our long journey which meant we lost, so we retreated back to Rome.

Alfred George Harvey Gillmore (9)
Olga Primary School, Tower Hamlets

The Queen Has Made A Friend

I am so excited! I got to meet the queen. But I had to take Lily with me, duh. She's my child. We were curtseying down the aisle. "Why does a gorilla have big nostrils? So it can fit its big fingers up there!" I blushed dark red. Why did Lily say that? Argh! I was so mad at her! One minute passed in silence, then I heard a shrill laugh. I checked if anyone was behind me. It was the queen! She was laughing at my child's jokes! That's how me and Queen Victoria became the best friends ever!

Stella Gessaroli (10)
Olga Primary School, Tower Hamlets

Hunted

As I ran from the soldiers, I heard my sister fall and stopped to help. "Run- " was all she managed to scream before it was cut off by a shot that rattled my ears. A single tear ran down my cheek as she took her last breath and I ran, diary held tight. I ran into the trees and I heard shots in the distance. I tripped on a branch, cutting my knee. I scrambled up and exited the trees. I stood until a hand pulled me behind cover. It was a kind Polish farmer. Safe. But, my diary wasn't...

Emmie Traversari (11)
Olga Primary School, Tower Hamlets

The Haunter Of Nightmares

It was big, it was cold-blooded, it was a huge sabre-toothed tiger! But not the normal one, it was chasing the dodo with speed and agility. The sabre-toothed monster caught up and sank its fangs into the bird's back and, finally, tossed it in the air, eating it. But, just then, the hero saw the beast and told it to fight him. The whole village showed up to watch, then the fight started. The beast went first, slashing its claws, but the hero dodged it. What would happen?

Caspian-James Leonard Phillips (10)
Olga Primary School, Tower Hamlets

The Mystery Of King Minos

It all began on the island of Crete. There was a small house on the coast and a young boy named Arthur. Arthur was fifteen and his family, the Lewises, were slaves of King Minos. They lived on little money and fought for their meek meals.
One morning, Arthur had had enough. He organised a rebellion against their tyrant king. Once they were ready, they began to plot. Stealthily, he retrieved the weaponry from the armoury. The young slaves rushed the soldiers. Arthur, enraged, assaulted the powerful yet sadistic King Minos. Arthur halted as he saw the shocking truth...

Ayman Mohamed (11)
Real Action Butterfly School, Queens Park

How Max The Dinosaur Got His Powers

Once, millions of years ago, a dinosaur roamed the universe. This is how he got his powers.

One stormy day, a meteor landed on a volcano, followed by a lightning bolt, then the volcano erupted. Just when the meteor was setting everything on fire, and all dinosaurs died except one called Max, Zeus appeared in the sky and gave Max powers. Max created all the dinosaurs. The day after, there was a heatwave and only one drop of water left, so Max teleported the dinosaurs to another planet, Pluto. The heatwave was one hundred degrees Celsius, the very, very end.

Nathan Melaka (7)
Real Action Butterfly School, Queens Park

The Great Dino War

4.5 billion years ago, dinosaurs were the kings of the planet. But, one god wanted to stop all dinosaur attacks. His name was Zikor, a powerful god who could use his powers to help the world, galaxy, universe or the whole Milky Way. The battle was extremely dangerous because it was a lot of dinosaurs versus one god. Zikor collected an army of gods but, in the middle of the battle, half of the dinos were nailed, making it an equal fight. Although, unfortunately, some gods were murdered or injured, Zikor used his powerful abilities and wiped out the dinosaurs...

Amir Azimi (10)
Real Action Butterfly School, Queens Park

The Mummy

Once upon a time, there was a lady called Mary. She lived in Eygpt. Once, she went to a secret place where there were mummies. Suddenly, a mummy placed her inside a dark, rusty tomb. After four days, a person named Alexa came. She heard screaming. She opened the tomb and saw Mary. She helped her out. Mary explained to Alexa what happened, so they tried to stop the mummy by creating a plan and it worked. They felt happy and stayed with each other until the mummy was buried and rose up again... but they had a great time.

Rebeca Mare (9)
Real Action Butterfly School, Queens Park

Florence Nightingale's Family

Florence Nightingale's dad had gotten very sick. Her father had been stressed from all the work he'd been doing and she decided to be more helpful than she was. Because she started to help her feather more, he got better. Because he thought he was better, he stood up and ran to Florence. He slipped and went to the hospital. Florence was tired. She still went to the hospital with him and the results were bad because when he slipped and fell on his head he lost a lot of blood and died. Her family went to sleep.

Yeabsira Tegenu (7)
Real Action Butterfly School, Queens Park

Cleopatra The Mighty Queen

It was another boring, hot day as Cleopatra, the mighty queen, sat on her throne. As she was sitting, she noticed a scroll next to her. It looked like one of those old, mysterious scrolls that were hard to get your hands on. *Wow!* thought Cleopatra to herself. Confused, she took the scroll to read what was inside. For five minutes, she read until she reached a point about the golden fountain of youth. Curiously, she lifted the next page and it began glowing. In a flash, she vanished into thin air...

Anamika Shaw (9)
Real Action Butterfly School, Queens Park

Toilet Roll

Once upon a time, a boy called Zeus was born. He had long hair and everyone loved him. When Zeus grew up, he became a responsible child. One day, he gave all his money to two hungry men who hadn't eaten in five days. When Zeus grew up, everyone worshipped him because of how nice and responsible he was. One day, a dragon came, attacking Zeus' village. All of a sudden, lightning hit Zeus, then he had so much energy, he went head-to-head with the dragon. Zeus put lightning on the dragon, then he died.

Alex Read (10)
Real Action Butterfly School, Queens Park

Egypt's Mummy

Once, there lived a man called Alex. He worked as a tomb cleaner. One day, he was cleaning a tomb of an ancient pharaoh. He opened it up to see if there were any cobwebs in the tomb and he saw a live mummy! The mummy sat up and climbed out of the tomb very slowly. He ran and ran while screaming for help. His legs were aching, his heart was pounding in his chest. His throat was burning. The mummy caught up and was about to grab him...

Naomi Kassa (9)
Real Action Butterfly School, Queens Park

Murder Mystery

Before time was made, I, Malaika, encountered a filthy murder in front of the dining room but, before any of that happened... I was on my way down when I heard an argument about who was going to be pharaoh. I listened secretly until I heard a scream. I hid amongst the statues to see who was killed. I looked and, with my own eyes, saw a filthy murder. Gazing at me was a lady. I didn't really get to look at her because she turned and ran away. I sprinted and realised it was Hatshepsut.

Malaika Raja (9)
Roe Green Junior School, Brent

The Run!

It was a dark, gloomy night. The streets were crowded with billions of people going into their bunkers.

My friend and I were on our way until we were caught in the bombing. We tried to find a bunker, but they were all taken. We were quivering with fear as we ran for our lives.

Anyway, as we were running, we encountered a massive tank! I ran as fast as I could, my friend was behind me and... *bang!* He fell...

My best friend died in the war...

Abdullah Ibnu Muhammad (9)
Roe Green Junior School, Brent

My Nightmare

Before time was recorded, I encountered a T-rex. Who would think this could occur in the jungle at noon? Believe me, neither did I! It was massive, terrifying and fierce. That was it. I wondered if this was the end of my journey. Looking into its eyes was like it was about to hypnotise me. By now, I escaped the terrifying and colossal T-rex. I ran as fast as I could and I escaped the disgusting and mysterious ancient jungle.

Shadar Wilson (9)
Roe Green Junior School, Brent

A Day Out With Henry Tudor

Walking into a small store, spitting on the floor, Henry Tudor commanded his meaningless servants to strip the store of their products. As they agreed in fear of the scary king, they grabbed every single thing they could see. Henry commanded them to take everything from the poor customers.

Helplessly, everyone hesitated to fight with him. But an old peasant woman was courageous enough to fight. "How dare you touch my stuff, you impolite man!"

"Man!" Henry shouted. "I am your mighty king! You will bow down to me!" As she refused, Henry threatened her with a gold dagger.

Tayyab Ahmed Hussain (10)
St James' CE Junior School, Forest Gate

The Story Of Henry The VIII's Wives

In the fifteenth century, there was Henry VIII. He married Catherine of Aragon. She was going to marry his brother but he died. They had a daughter but divorced. Then he decided to marry Anne Boleyn and she got beheaded because she promised she would have a son but never did. Henry's next wife died because Jane got sick after giving birth. Next was Anne of Cleves. They divorced because she had no children. His next wife got beheaded because Catherine was beautiful but cold-hearted on the inside. Lastly, there was Catherine Parr who survived because Henry died before her.

Aleena Ahmed (10)
St James' CE Junior School, Forest Gate

Boudicca Vs Rome

Long ago, in the ancient times, I saw this lady called Boudicca. She was the wife of Prasutagus. He was the ruler of the Iceni tribes. But when he died, Boudicca became the leader of the Iceni tribe. The Romans were marching to the Iceni tribe. "Why are they here? Attack!" said Boudicca. Boudicca jumped on a horse and, while she was running with the horse, she was fighting Romans with her sharp, pointy sword. The Romans won and took over the whole Iceni lands. Boudicca was heartbroken and anxious because she didn't win so she left the Iceni tribe.

Tahreema Jwardar (9)
St James' CE Junior School, Forest Gate

Crazy Julius Caesar

Many years ago, there was a Roman leader called Julius Caesar. He was training his army to fight against Britain. The army kept training against each other. They trained day and night to prepare themselves to defeat Britain, their biggest enemy country. As they were ready, they climbed hill after hill until they got to Celtic land and attacked the British. Suddenly, they noticed their leader was gone. The Celts took Julius Caesar and were about to kill him but he was sleeping for no reason and was dreaming of black sheep chasing him. He was just truly crazy!

Jihan Waasil (9)
St James' CE Junior School, Forest Gate

Untitled

Once upon a time, there was a Roman emperor called Julius Caesar and he had a big nose and a big army at his disposal. Also, he had a wife.
"Now, I'm going to defeat the British Celts and steal the land!" But, Boudicca didn't let them take the land. She fought the Romans and won.
"C'mon, we can't get beaten by a girl, we are better than this!" argued Caesar.
They tried to get over the marshes but they got stuck so the Celts won again.
"I give up, you win!" said Caesar, so the Celts won.

Aritz Ayomikun Akinrele (8)
St James' CE Junior School, Forest Gate

Missing Mummy!

"Unfortunately, the day has arrived where the pharaoh's glory days are over with us. It is time to say goodbye and take him to his tomb. We should let him enjoy his afterlife with what he has!"
The day after his mummification, his slaves went to see him for the very last time but, instead, they found an unpleasant surprise... the pharaoh was missing... or should I say, the mummy was missing. He was nowhere to be found in his tomb with his luxuries. All that was left were his organs but where had our beloved pharaoh's body gone?

Eliza Emini (11)
St James' CE Junior School, Forest Gate

Escape Of The Mummy!

Suddenly, the woods shook. I froze, paralysed with absolute fear. I inched my head backwards, taking shallow breaths, consumed with fear. When I saw the beast, my jaw dropped in shock and my throat released a raspy splutter. A mummy stood behind me. It had eyes like lava, teeth black as the night and released a foul stench. I barbarically ran in any direction, my eyes trying to escape. Suddenly, I clumsily tripped. I saw the mummy limping towards me, a barbaric smile on its face. I shut my eyes, my body rigid in absolute fear. There was no escape...

Fabia Isabele Svetlikauskaite (10)
St James' CE Junior School, Forest Gate

Victorian Childhood

It was a normal day in Victorian life. Most of the children went to school but the rich were homeschooled. I've heard that the children have horrible childhoods so I'm going to be interviewing a Victorian child named Anastasia.

"So, Anastasia, how do you find school?"

"As I'm a poor child, I don't like it because we get treated so badly. Also, I have to do many chores like factory-working, chimney-sweeping and more!" Anastasia cried.

"Thank you, Anastasia, for sharing your daily life with us!"

Arianna Ahmed (11)
St James' CE Junior School, Forest Gate

The Magical King

Long ago lived an Egyptian king called Tutankhamun who was blessed thanks to the god Anubis who gave him beautiful, golden treasure. The powerful god gave him so much treasure that everyone tried to steal from Tutankhamun. So, to make sure nothing was stolen, Anubis hid the tomb and pyramid so nothing could be taken but a man called Howard Carter and Lord Carnarvon found the tomb, but tomb robbers came as well. So, they fought and Tutankhamun rose from the dead and cursed the tomb thieves and left Howard Carter and Lord Carnarvon healthy again.

Ihsaan Mujaddid Uzzaman (8)
St James' CE Junior School, Forest Gate

Bipidy Bopady Boo, Bringing A Mummy Back To Life

There was once a young Egyptian princess who loved experimenting with the dead. Each time, something new would happen. As a kid, she was never scared of anything. She would get all sorts of liquids and pour them on the dead mummies. One day, she had a warning saying, "Do not ever go to the Nile..." But, being a greedy, selfish girl, she didn't listen and went on, curious. She took a sample of the Nile and decided to put it on the mummies to see what would happen. She got the Nile water and poured it. The mummy rose!

Rose Boadi (11)
St James' CE Junior School, Forest Gate

The Spanish Armada

As I marched onto the boat in Kent, I realised I could see the Armada. Almost. Suddenly, I was at sea. The Spanish enemy had a villainous leader called King Philip II. His aim was to rule England. I tried to focus by standing still. The Armada was firing. I focused for a second, endlessly firing at the Armada. All of a sudden, a storm came and wrecked all of the boats from the Armada's army. Sir Francis Drake was correct. He was very smart and a good man. He helped England. Ultimately, the extensive and tiring battle ended.

Bubacari Dembaga (10)
St James' CE Junior School, Forest Gate

Julius Caesar

Once upon an unpleasant time, there was a man called Julius Caesar. He was a fierce, strong Roman emperor who actually was wealthy and smart. Anyway, let me tell you his story. Julius Caesar loved watching the gladiators fight. I think one of the reasons he loved watching them fight was because he could decide if they would win or not. He could see it best because he was sat on the podium. One day, Julius Caesar was assassinated by his friends, so that basically meant he was betrayed by his friends. Then Augustus took over!

Ismail Muhammad (10)
St James' CE Junior School, Forest Gate

What Actually Happened With King Henry The VIII

Around 1510, in England, there was a horrible king, Henry VIII. He wished for a boy so when he died, he would be king. With hope, Henry married Katya, he wasn't lucky. He divorced her by making the Church of England. He married a second wife. I don't think he even liked her, he beheaded her. Thankfully, the third wife gave birth to a boy. Unfortunately, she died. The fourth wife was divorced (not a shock). The next wife was the most gruesome one, she was beheaded. The final wife magically survived out of six wives!

Hajar Bennebri (10)
St James' CE Junior School, Forest Gate

The Pharaoh And The Mummy

Once, there was a pharaoh called Jack and his wife called Victoria and they had children. They also had a dog. Their family was always happy. Then the pharaoh saw a walking mummy! The mummy was so rude. Then they were sleeping at night. Then the mummy had a knife in his hand. The mummy went into the huge pharaoh's castle. He wanted to kill the whole entire family. Then the pharaoh angrily chased the mummy. The pharaoh gave him one last chance or else he would kill the mummy. He killed him and they were happy again.

Amirah Mahreen Begum (8)
St James' CE Junior School, Forest Gate

The Horrible Henry VIII

Back in 1509, Henry ruled terrible England. Horrible Henry was not nice to anyone who lived in England. Henry had six wives, he wanted a son before he died so his son could be the next king. His first wife was divorced so Henry had to destroy the Catholic church. The second wife was beheaded, the third wife died, the fourth was divorced, the fifth was beheaded and the sixth survived and Henry died. There were no kings but there was a Queen Elizabeth who ruled England and she had a sister called Mary who married Philip.

Caleb Barnieh (10)
St James' CE Junior School, Forest Gate

Back In Victorian Times

There was a girl called Rose, she loved life. Later on in the evening, when Rose was getting tucked in by her mum and dad, she fell asleep and woke up in dull Victorian times. Rose had a problem, she didn't know how to get back home. Then everybody was saying she was queen. "Where is she?" Rose said, "Wait, I'm queen! This must be a dream!" She ran off, then she saw that she was a grown-up. When she looked at the streets, she saw that people were wearing dresses. Then she was in bed again.

Aniyah Wilson Opoku (9)
St James' CE Junior School, Forest Gate

The Victorious Country!

Once, there was a mean prince called Prince Philip who ruled over Spain, Portugal, part of Italy and many more. Philip's wife, Mary, had died, so now he wanted to marry Queen Elizabeth because he wanted to rule England. Elizabeth refused to marry him. She made a great choice. Philip became angry, so he got the Spanish Armada to attack England. There was a captain called Francis Drake and he knew that the wind would blow their enemies in the opposite direction. England won! Hooray! Another victory for England.

Ashmal Khan (10)
St James' CE Junior School, Forest Gate

King Henry VIII And His Six Wives

In 1509, Henry VIII began his reign as king of England. He had six wives, their names were Catherine of Aragon, Anne Boleyn, Catherine Howard, Anne of Cleves, Jane Seymour and Catherine Parr. However, before it came to him divorcing some of his wives, he had to form a new church called the Church of England. Once he did that, people were allowed to divorce. All thanks to Jane Seymour, he had a son called Edward. He was nicknamed Sir Edward Seymour, the Protector. But sadly he died on January 22nd 1552 in London.

Soloman Rehan (10)
St James' CE Junior School, Forest Gate

Stuck In The Stone Age

Tom was making the best time machine ever! He thought it would be the best. By the time he was finished, he tested it out straight away. So he typed in where he wanted to go. 'Modern-Day Paris, 2030'. But he forgot to make the motor, so it reversed it to go to Italy, 7500 BC, the Stone Age. Tom was really surprised when he got there. As he was exploring, he met a Stone Age man who agreed to help him fix his machine. When he finished fixing it, Tom shouted, "Home sweet home!" and he was home!

Ivet Penovska (8)

St James' CE Junior School, Forest Gate

Spartacus The Gladiator!

Long ago, there used to be a Roman slave called
Spartacus. They arrested him and put him in the
Colosseum to perform. He was so worried that
someone would kill him in the fight to the death.
From that day on, he trained to be the best.
One sunny evening, he was shaking in his boots.
He was sweating as if he was attacked by a tiger.
"Argh!" yelled Mrs Mehmoohd. He ran and gave
her a spear to kill the lion.
"Roar!" cried the lion. He was so relieved. But, the
emperor was so angry!

Saifan Khan (9)
St James' CE Junior School, Forest Gate

The Six Wives

It was 1519, when Henry VIII was ruling England. He thought if he had a wife, he would have a son. But Henry only had one son. Sadly, when Henry was married to Anne of Cleves, he realised she was ugly, so he divorced her. His other wife was Lucy, she survived his horrible evilness but after, she sadly died. Henry's daughter, Queen Elizabeth, was also very bad. She didn't like a man called Philip who was the king of Spain. The queen didn't like him at all, so she stole from him and he was angry.

Andrea Boateng (10)

St James' CE Junior School, Forest Gate

Romulus And Remus

One morning, there were twins with their mother.
Their mother was very sick and looked like she was
going to die. Sadly, she had to throw them into the
river because of that. Fortunately, a magnificent,
caring she-wolf picked them out of the river. The
she-wolf was was like a mother to the twins as she
took care of them. Suddenly, they saw their
grandpa die.
One day, Romulus and Remus had a terrible fight
over which hill they should build a city on. Their
father died because the twins killed him.

Russell Casey Addotey (9)
St James' CE Junior School, Forest Gate

The Mummy Came Alive!

Long ago in ancient Egypt, there lived a queen, glamorous Luna. She lived in a hot, burning desert which was called the Kingdom of the Magical Sands. One day, she decided to make meat with lots of spices to feed her special mummy who was in a dark tomb. When she arrived, the mummy suddenly came to life and menacingly approached her. She was so terrified. She ran across the golden sands, screaming. She kept running until handsome King Liver heard her and saved her. They became best friends forever.

Liyana Haque (8)
St James' CE Junior School, Forest Gate

Divorced, Beheaded, Died

Henry VIII was a handsome king but he had issues as a king. His first wife, Catherine, was divorced. Henry VIII had five other wives. His second wife, Anne Boleyn, got beheaded because she lost a baby and therefore got beheaded. His third wife died but Henry loved her and, when he died, his grave was put next to his third wife, Jane Seymour. His fourth wife, Anne of Cleves, was divorced like Catherine of Aragon. Catherine Howard was the fifth wife of Henry VIII, she was also beheaded by Henry.

Matyas Sarosi (10)
St James' CE Junior School, Forest Gate

Bella And Jack

Once upon a time, there was a girl called Bella and Bella took three hundred miles to go to ancient Egypt by car. When she got there, she saw a big pyramid and pharaohs. They checked on the car and Bella was very sad because she'd have to walk forty thousand miles home. But, before they went, they explored a little bit and saw some treasure in a deep pyramid. Then they went back home for dinner. Just in time, they found out what happened to their car and they learned about the treasure.

Ramaiya Princess Payne Fearon (8)
St James' CE Junior School, Forest Gate

Egyptians Roam

Once, in the hot desert, there was an Egyptian pharaoh who was on his way home when some mummies seemed mad. They were servants that went to the afterlife. He said, "It's great to see you again!" but then they chased him. He hid, he couldn't get rid of them, so he traded some gold to be free. They made a deal so the pharaoh was free. He carried on and tried to go home without getting hurt or bruised. At that moment, he couldn't see his house but then he saw his house.

Edward Osie Kwame (8)
St James' CE Junior School, Forest Gate

Scary Ancient Egypt

One day, there was a queen called Sitoma, she lived in ancient Egypt and she lived with a pharaoh and a mummy. One day, the mummy started walking and he kept on causing trouble. The queen found out, so the queen started spying on him and, finally, the queen caught the mummy and killed him. The queen took all the mummy's jewellery and the queen became the richest queen on the Earth and she became famous. People from all over the Earth visited ancient Egypt and stayed there forever.

Aleena Hoque (8)
St James' CE Junior School, Forest Gate

The Big Pyramid

Once upon a time, there was an ancient priest who was bored out of his mind. Then he said, "What shall I do? I'm bored! Who wants a rest?" The problem was, there was a servant, his name was Thone. He saw the priest and the workers having a rest, so the servant shouted, "What are you doing?" At last, they all worked together and made a big pyramid and a statue. It was also made out of sand bricks. The servant, Thone, was helping. They were helping each other!

Hima Subair (9)

St James' CE Junior School, Forest Gate

The Shutdown!

I, Henry VIII, had been thinking, *All that land, gone, just because of those annoying monasteries. I know what to do! I'll shut them all down.* I left with a friend and took them down one by one. I said to them, "If you take care of poor people, I will behead you!" They got so scared that they scattered. To this day, I still have them as slaves. Most of them died, but I don't care! As for my friend, he died for betraying me and protecting the monasteries.

Anayet Noor (10)
St James' CE Junior School, Forest Gate

The Secret Gold Stash

One normal day, I was cleaning for King Henry as usual. I was always tired and fed up. Later that day, I was dusting the floor and a secret passage opened and there was a load of pure, shiny gold. I went down but suddenly the door shut behind me. I was worried about how to get out but first I got all the gold underground. I got bags and bags, then I just had to get out. Luckily, I found a key which opened the secret passage and then I went on to become the richest Tudor alive!

Kayla Monica Monteiro (10)
St James' CE Junior School, Forest Gate

Ancient Henry VIII

Back centuries ago, there lived Henry VIII. He was desperate for a son. He married but couldn't divorce or get a son. So, Henry changed the law and divorced her. Then, his third wife couldn't give him a son. He beheaded her. Henry's fourth wife didn't give him a son. He was furious. So, he beheaded her. Henry's fifth wife was beheaded. With hope, Henry married Jane. After all that, Jane gave Henry a son. Henry, Jane and their son lived happily ever after.

Nisha Kaur (10)
St James' CE Junior School, Forest Gate

The Dissolution

Henry VIII was the rudest of all. He had six wives, the first one was Catherine. She gave him a lovely daughter called Mary Tudor but, sadly, she didn't give Henry a son. Henry was cross so he wanted to do something. He divorced her but it didn't work out so he tried to be the owner of a very cool place, the church. After a few more days, Henry was exhausted. When his wife died, he was very lonely in the world and he had no one to talk to but he still had some money.

Maria Camila Galarza (10)
St James' CE Junior School, Forest Gate

The Mummies Are Out!

It was very late at night in Egypt. I had been sleeping until a loud *thud* had woken me up. I slowly stepped out of bed and grabbed my torch. Trying my best not to wake anyone up, I stepped out the house. As I was walking out, I switched my torch on to see what that loud thud was. I saw something near the pyramids, so I went all the way down. When I arrived at the pyramids, I saw rolls of tissue. I followed it until it came to an end. I soon realised it was a mummy!

Aysha Begum (11)
St James' CE Junior School, Forest Gate

The Kingdom Of The Tombs

In the Kingdom of the Tombs, on the hot, nice sands lived a queen and a pharaoh and a cat. They were bored. Then Queen Perl said, "I have an idea, let's go on an adventure!" Then they went to a cool place called the Tombs. They went inside the tombs and they saw a big, huge tomb and inside it was a mummy. Everyone ran as fast as they could and they found another mummy. "What can we do?" said Queen Perl. Then they drank a potion and went back home.

Perla Alegra Petkeviciute (7)
St James' CE Junior School, Forest Gate

The Wild Adventures

First, there was a boy who went on an aeroplane to Egypt. He arrived but suddenly he forgot to buy another ticket to go home. So he lived in ancient Egypt. Then he saw the Tower of Pisa, some pyramids, hieroglyphs and a sarcophagus! Also, he saw Carter, who found the first sarcophagus. Carter found a time machine to go to the future, so he went in. Just when he was about to pull the lever, his phone rang. But, nobody called. Then some guards shot them and killed them.

Jojo Sam (8)
St James' CE Junior School, Forest Gate

Tyrese Jones' Adventure!

A boy called Tyrese loved an Emperor called Claudius because he was destructive as hell. He designed a time watch for himself so he could travel back in time. Soon, he started working on it. After that, he completed the time watch. Then Tyrese tested it. All of a sudden, he travelled to a Roman battle. He watched how the Romans battled the warriors. Next, the warriors froze and looked at him. They threw their spears at him! Luckily, he went back to the normal world!

Tyrese Henry (8)
St James' CE Junior School, Forest Gate

The Portal

Once upon a time, there was a boy called Sargeant Jonathon Phillip. He worked for the West Midlands Police. One day, he found a portal. As soon as he went in, he found dinosaurs and volcanoes. Then he looked up in the air, he saw a giant rock, it had fire on it. That scared him a lot. It was coming closer. As soon as it hit the Earth, it killed all of the dinosaurs. He saw the portal. When he went through, he was back in his office. He carried on with his work.

Daniel Mazose (8)
St James' CE Junior School, Forest Gate

The Travel Pharaoh

One very hot day, the pharaoh went inside a weird box. He travelled to the moon and went inside the moon. He tried to move but it was no use. He yelled for help, he yelled his friends' names but nothing happened. Then he found cheese everywhere. He also found out the weird box was still there, so he could go back and come back. The next day, he went back and sold all the cheese he could find and that is how ancient Egyptians became famous for cheese!

Alisa Emini (8)
St James' CE Junior School, Forest Gate

Roman Gladiators In The Colosseum

A long time ago, there were gladiators that battled to death and, whoever won, the judge would decide, a thumbs up or down. His name was Caus, he was tall and powerful. Once, I went to the battle. I was terrified because I thought I would die and the other gladiator was going to win. Then, he didn't win, I won and I was happy. Then I became a Roman soldier for twenty years. I was rewarded with money and was a normal person with the best family ever!

Mantas Kairys (9)
St James' CE Junior School, Forest Gate

Queen Elizabeth I

Once, there was a lady called Queen Elizabeth, she was very unattractive. She also had a cousin called Mary who lived in Scotland, she was once queen but since Queen Elizabeth was super jealous (which was ridiculous) she sent people to go and find Mary and bring her to the queen. Mary never knew that Queen Elizabeth was coming. A few hours later, they found her and she was beheaded and died. That was very sorrowful and it was also very cruel!

Manuela Tami Adamu Adegbenro (10)
St James' CE Junior School, Forest Gate

Tudor Tragedy

Long, long ago, there lived the horrible Tudors. Henry VIII was the vilest of them all. He ruled with six wives, two that were beheaded and one that survived. All he ever wished was to have a boy but the majority of his wives served him with a girl. He could not keep his anger inside. Henry VIII did not fear at all. He would murder everyone who disobeyed him. The Tudor tragedy was a moment for some to never forget.

Aisha Saddiq (10)
St James' CE Junior School, Forest Gate

Elizabeth And Philip

Once upon a time, Philip, the king of Spain and the leader of the Spanish Armada, wanted to take over Britain. So, first, he wanted to do it the easy way and marry Elizabeth I, who was the queen of England. But, that didn't work, so he tried to attack Britain in his best formation but they couldn't attack because there wasn't enough space to attack like that, so they retreated and forgot about Britain.

Rahell Noori (10)
St James' CE Junior School, Forest Gate

Stone Age

One day, the Stone Age began. On the first day the world began in time, people were floating around and they landed on Earth. Then they woke up in a dump and made friends. They had an idea for the Stone Age and kept on hunting and hunting to make sticks with flint. Flint was the sharpest thing in the Stone Age, they used it to kill animals and eat them. Then, one day, the Bronze Age began and the Stone Age ended.

Farhan Omar Kazi (8)
St James' CE Junior School, Forest Gate

The Supreme Leader

King Henry VIII took over all of the monasteries. He did it to divorce one of his wives as the monks wouldn't let him. Now, Henry VIII was the supreme leader. But then, one monk in one of the monasteries told him what religion was really about and Henry gave all the monasteries back. He also became a better king and more religious.

Yahyah Islam (10)
St James' CE Junior School, Forest Gate

Jupiter's Jewels

High above the skies, mighty, muscular Jupiter stood, eyeballing the galaxy's five most precious, powerful crystals. An array of frightening gods surrounded him as millions of arrows came blasting down from the heavens. Pegasus, his horse, screeched in frustration. The jewels were out of their reach. From the clouds high above in the heavens, Jupiter's loyal eagle swooped down and snatched the jewels with his talons as sharp as kitchen knives. He soared towards Jupiter, dropping the jewels into the palm of the owner. Jupiter's muscled bulged and the other gods stepped away in awe. They trembled with fear...

Adam Bogdanowicz Bower (8)
St John's Highbury Vale, Highbury

My Home Is A Pyramid

I am going to tell you about the most epic time I had when I climbed a pyramid. An old man had offered me a house for ten shillings. I was suspicious of him, but I really needed a house. Mine was scruffy and ugly, so I accepted. We walked eight miles to the house. The man said the house was the tall pyramid. He then sauntered away. I wanted to climb it and I got to the top! Then I fell. I looked at the mummies. They opened the box and started walking towards me. They were alive!

Ryan Laurent Xavier Ssimbwa (10)
St Mark's CE Primary School, Lambeth

A Chess Game

My brain was bursting with stress and my thoughts were all over the place. I entered the chess competition with all the best-trained players of Mesopotamia. I was determined to make my father happy. He had never shown a smile since he was wounded in battle. My heart was frozen and I stood still when I found my father in the Ziggurat with an eyepatch. My mother was a noblewoman. When I'm older, I'll fight fiercely, fearlessly, ferociously, deadly, viciously, mercilessly and I'll give revenge to the city that left an eternal scar on my father.

Thomas Bignone (9)
St Nicholas School, Brent

A Farmer's Failure

One scorching hot day in Mesopotamia, a lonely farmer stood proudly in the middle of his glorious field. His electric-blue eyes were full of cruel kindness as they danced around their sockets. He stared at his gorgeous flowers and they smelt fabulous! The king's crops were also divine. In the corner of his eye, he saw a raging cow who was destroying the crops at a rapid pace. The farmer cursed deafeningly in his new language. The king would torture him now. The cow was so annoying. His heart was beating swiftly. Was this his final breath, was it?

Mayon Wanniarachchige (10)
St Nicholas School, Brent

A Day Unlike Any Before

I woke up to another day and, I must say, it was different, very different. The air was sweet, the houses square, surrounded by deep, yellow fields so fair. The river ran by my feet so clear that a reflection was seen. The king and his writers were on the free side, the slaves behind them, walking by. The land of the two rivers, alive and well, hoping to discover time, writing and the wheel as well! *Bang! Bang!* This new thing comes, they call them drums. Oh, wait, there are more, it is the wonderful, beautiful and graceful harp!

Jumana Mahmud (10)
St Nicholas School, Brent

King Tut's Discovery

Days of frustration, days of anger. Lord Carnarvon shouted at Howard Carter while looking for the tomb of Tutankhamun. Searching all over Egypt, Tutankhamun still wasn't found.

After months and years of digging, still nothing was seen of the young ruler. Finally, on a day of luck and happiness, the nine-year-old king's tomb was found by the famous archaeologist, Howard Carter. He was amazed by the wonderful treasures of King Tut; jewellery, gold, silver brightened the tomb. Rotten and dirty, the king was very old, not nice to touch. The tomb, full of mud and dirt, was finally discovered.

George Christodoulou (8)
St Paul's CE Primary School, Winchmore Hill

Harsh Times

Elmo was terrified, Caesar would not be happy. The Roman guards dragged the slave back to the dangerous Colosseum, where Elmo knew this would be his last day. The arena was covered in sand and surrounded by thousands of seats. Tonight, an excited audience would fill them. Elmo felt nervous and anxious. The army general, Caesar, was furious, "Take him to the pit!" The pits were rough and smelly and all around him, glaring red eyes stared straight at Elmo. His time had come. Elmo was alone, until the savage lion was released and the audience gasped in fear...

Isaac Dempsey (9)
St Paul's CE Primary School, Winchmore Hill

The Treasure In The Pyramid

"Look, I found a secret door! We're in the pyramid!"
We are treasure hunters. We heard a rumour that
there was treasure in the pyramid. "Let's split into
two groups!" When I was walking nervously, I heard
a voice.

"Help me!" I approached slowly, feeling terrified.
When I opened the door, there was lots of treasure.
When I opened the big box, there was an ancient
Egyptian cadaver. When we tried to run away, I
saw a mummy coming towards us. We sprinted
faster at the last moment. That mummy is still
wandering around in the pyramid.

Osuke Ueda (10)
The Japanese School in London, Acton

Mummy In The Pyramid

My family and I visited Egypt on holiday and went on a tour to see inside the towering, triangular, grave pyramid. While I was looking at the scruffy wall, I felt something strange and I thought something might be behind the wall. I looked back towards where we were walking but no one was there. I was lost. I frantically searched for the way out through a dark corridor. I crept slowly, looking around nervously. Then I heard a footstep coming towards me. A silhouette appeared with a loose bandage around its body. It was a gruesome, limping mummy...

Julie Marumoto (9)
The Japanese School in London, Acton

Magnus And The Lion

Magnus got pushed out into the Colosseum. He could see about ten thousand people and a terrifying lion. It had claws like knives, eyes as dark as a thousand midnights and teeth dripping blood. The guard said to Magnus, "The lion has killed twelve men before!"

But Magnus said, "Well, I killed five bears and a wolf!" The battle started. They were face-to-face. Magnus was old and tired but he was very brave and he did not give up. He only had an old sword. The lion dove and Magnus threw the sword as hard as he could...

Joseph Duxbury (9)
The Japanese School in London, Acton

Cleopatra Is A Dinosaur!

I went to Egypt. I didn't have a map so I lost my way. Suddenly, I saw a secret door and Cleopatra appeared. Cleopatra said, "I will take you to the dinosaur age. If we go through the secret door, we can go anywhere!"
I said, "I want to go!"
We went through the secret door. In a flash, I reached the dinosaur age. Cleopatra went near the dinosaurs and talked with them. "I'm speaking with the dinosaur because I'm a dinosaur!" I was so surprised! I didn't know Cleopatra was a dinosaur!

Chika Tsunoda (10)
The Japanese School in London, Acton

The Enchanted Doll's House

One autumn day, I was playing with my new doll's house. As I was trying to open one of the doors, a sudden gust of wind came and swept me off my feet. When I landed, I was in a magnificent Victorian room. I wore a beautiful gown. In front of me was a Victorian doll's house. I felt peculiar but happy.

Suddenly, one of the doors opened and a doll my size came to life. I screamed as I tore down the corridor, straight into the garden. "Go away!" I yelled.

Miraculously, I was safely back home with Mum.

Aiko Groves (9)
The Japanese School in London, Acton

The Scary Mummy!

In the dusty desert, there was a tiny pyramid. Inside was sparse. However, there was one creepy coffin and a strange stick. I went inside and removed the stick. Then there was a rumble and a tumble. A high-pitched sound came from the coffin. The lid opened and a mummy crept out. I stepped back so she wouldn't get me. She was bleeding all over her body. I tried to put it back but it broke in half. There was no escape. I ran very fast. Unfortunately, the mummy scratched my whole body. Then I became a zombie!

Minori Muramatsu (9)
The Japanese School in London, Acton

Ice Age

Long, long ago, it was the mammoth age. It was the Ice Age. People who lived in the village moved because they couldn't live during the Ice Age. However, it was said that the mammoths were strong enough and heavy enough against the cold to end the Ice Age. So the kind people asked a mammoth to help them end the Ice Age. Finally, the mammoth came on top of the ice and jumped. It was so heavy that the continent was blown away, so that's why the current continents look the way they do.

Mai Akakura (10)
The Japanese School in London, Acton

The Rumbling Noise

I was outside in the woods. I heard a big rumbling noise. The wind blew as the lightning was flashing. Suddenly, the rocks shook and the sand blew across the ocean. I took out my torch and raised it up to the sky. There was a giant golem staring straight at me. I was frightened, so I tried to escape. Unfortunately, it caught my right arm. I screamed. Suddenly, I became a golem too. I was terribly sad. I just wanted to go home to my parents. I will never go to the woods on my own again.

Kyo Adachi Mavromichalis (9)
The Japanese School in London, Acton

YOUNG WRITERS INFORMATION

We hope you have enjoyed reading this book – and that you will continue to in the coming years.

If you're a young writer who enjoys reading and creative writing, or the parent of an enthusiastic poet or story writer, do visit our website www.youngwriters.co.uk. Here you will find free competitions, workshops and games, as well as recommended reads, a poetry glossary and our blog.

If you would like to order further copies of this book, or any of our other titles give us a call or visit **www.youngwriters.co.uk**.

Young Writers
Remus House
Coltsfoot Drive
Peterborough
PE2 9BF

(01733) 890066
info@youngwriters.co.uk

 YoungWritersUK

 @YoungWritersCW